Praise for *Looking Through Lace*

"... 'Looking Through Lace' by Ruth Nestvold [is] an intelligent, complex story illustrating the difficulties of learning and understanding the nuances and intricacies of an alien language and culture, particularly one so similar to our own that we persist in viewing it (wrongly) on our terms.... The reason ... why there are so many differences between the languages of both men and women are logical and well thought out, and the final revelation about the true nature of the relationship between the women and the men comes as a nice twist."

Phil Friel in *Tangent Online*

"'Looking Through Lace' by Ruth Nestvold is terrific science fiction. I want to read more of this writer's stories. The valuing/devaluing of 'women's work' is a theme here that is told well: not trite, not heavy, making a valid point while showing me an alien culture that was captivating from the first moment. It all worked."

Andi Shechter in *January Magazine*

LOOKING THROUGH LACE

Book I

Ruth Nestvold

Red Dragon Books

RUTH NESTVOLD

Publisher's Note: This is a work of fiction. Names, characters, places, and incidents are a product of the author's imagination. Locales and public names are sometimes used for atmospheric purposes. Any resemblance to actual people, living or dead, or to businesses, companies, events, institutions, or locales is completely coincidental.

Book Layout ©2014 BookDesignTemplates.com and Ruth Nestvold

Cover Design by Lou Harper. Image credit: NASA, ESA, the Hubble SM4 ERO Team, and The Hubble Heritage Team (STScI/AURA)

Looking Through Lace / Ruth Nestvold -- 1st printing
ISBN 978-1522730699

Originally published in *Asimov's* in 2003, "Looking Through Lace" was a finalist for the Tiptree and Sturgeon awards. The Italian translation won the *Premio Italia* for best work of speculative fiction in translation in 2007.

[1]

Toni came out of the jump groggy and with a slight headache, wishing the Allied Interstellar Research Association could afford passage on Alcubierre drive ships — even if they did collapse an unconscionable amount of space in their wake. For a moment, she couldn't remember what the job was this time. She sat up and rubbed her eyes while the voice on the intercom announced that they would be arriving at the Sagittarius Transit Station in approximately one standard hour.

Sagittarius. Now she remembered. The women's language. Suddenly she felt much more awake. For the first time, she was on her way to join a first contact team, and she had work to do. She got up, washed her face in cold water at the basin in her compartment (at least AIRA could afford private compartments), and turned on the console again, calling up the files she had been sent when given her assignment to Christmas.

"List vids," she said. It was time she checked her theoretical knowledge against the real thing again. Just over three weeks she'd had to learn the Megan language, one week on Admetos after getting her new assignment and two weeks in transit. From the transit station, it would be another week before she finally set foot on the planet. Even with the latest memory enhancements, it was a daunting challenge. A month to learn a new language and its intricacies. A month to try to get a feel for a culture where women had their own language which they never spoke with men.

That had been her lucky break. Toni was the only female xenolinguist in this part of the galaxy with more than a year's experience. And suddenly she found herself promoted from grunt, compiling grammars and dictionaries, to first contact team.

She scrolled through the list of vids. This time, she noticed a title which hadn't caught her attention before.

"Play 'Unknown Mejan water ritual.'"

To judge by the AIC date, it had to be a video from one of the early, pre-contact-team probes. Not to mention the quality, which was only sporadically focused. The visuals were mostly of the bay of Edaru, and the audio was dominated by the sound of water lapping the shore.

But what she could see and hear was fascinating. A fearful young hominid male, tall and gracile, his head shaved and bowed, was being led out by two guards to the end of a pier. A small crowd followed solemnly. When they arrived at the end, another man stepped forward and, in the only words Toni could make out clearly, announced that Sentalai's shame would be purged. (Assuming, of course, that what had been deciphered of the men's language to this point was correct.)

The older man then motioned for the younger man to remove his clothes, fine leather garments such as those worn by the richer of the Edaru clans, and when he was naked, the two guards pushed him into the water.

Three women behind them conferred briefly. Then one of the three stepped forward and flung a length of lace after the young man.

Toni stared as the crowd on the pier walked back to shore. She could see no trace of the man who had been thrown in the water. According to her materials, the Mejan were excellent swimmers, growing up nearly as much in the water as out, and it should have been easy for him to swim back to the pier. But for some reason he hadn't.

It reminded her of nothing so much as an execution.

[2]

The entry bay of the small space station orbiting Christmas was empty and sterile, with none of the personal details that a place accumulated with time, the details that made it lived-in rather than just in use. Toni was glad she would soon be moving to the planet's surface. Blank walls were more daunting than an archaic culture and an unknown language anytime.

Two men were there to meet her, and neither one was the team xenolinguist.

The elder of the two stepped forward, his hand outstretched. "Welcome to the *Penthesilea*, Dr. Donato."

"Thank you, Captain Ainsworth. It's a pleasure

to meet you. And please, call me Toni."

Ainsworth smiled but didn't offer his own first name in exchange. Hierarchies were being established quickly.

"Toni, this is Dr. Samuel Wu, the new xenoteam sociologist."

From their vid communications, Toni had expected to like Sam Wu, and now she was sure of it. His smile was slow and sincere and his handshake firm. Besides, he was in a similar position on the team, having been brought into the project late after the original sociologist, Landra Saleh, had developed a serious intolerance to something in the atmosphere of Christmas, despite the battery of tests they all went through before being assigned to a new planet.

"Nice to meet you in person, Toni," Sam said.

"Nice to meet you too." Toni looked from one to the other. "And Dr. Repnik? Was he unable to leave the planet?"

There was a short silence. "Uh, he thought Dr. Wu could brief you on anything that has come up since the last communication you received. Continued study of the language has precedence at this point."

Toni nodded. "Of course." But that didn't change

the fact that another xenolinguist could brief her better than a sociologist — especially one who had only been on the planet a week himself.

As Ainsworth led her to her quarters aboard ship, she drew Sam aside. "Okay, what's all this about?"

"I was afraid you'd notice," he said, grimacing.

"And?"

"I guess it's only fair that you know what you'll be up against. Repnik didn't think a female linguist needed to be added to the team, but Ainsworth insisted on it."

Toni sighed. She had been looking forward to working with Repnik. Of the dozen inhabited worlds discovered in the last century, he'd been on the xenoteams of half of them and had been the initial xenolinguist on three. He had more experience in making sense of unknown languages than anyone alive. And the languages of Christmas were a fascinating puzzle, a puzzle she'd thought she would get a chance to work on with one of the greatest xenolinguists in the galaxy. Instead, she would be a grunt again — an unwanted grunt.

"Here we are," Ainsworth said, as the door to one of the cabins opened at his touch. "We'll have the entrance reprogrammed as soon as you settle in."

"Thank you."

"We'll be going planetside tomorrow. I hope that's enough time for you to recover from your journey."

It never was, but it was all she was going to get. "I'm sure I'll be fine."

"Good, then I will leave you with Dr. Wu so that he can brief you on anything you still need to know."

She set her bag down on the narrow bed and gazed out the viewport at the planet. It was a a striking sight. The discovery team that had done the first fly-by of the Sgr 132 solar system had given it the name Christmas. The vegetation was largely shades of red and the ocean had a greenish cast, while the narrow band of rings alternated shades of green and gold. There was only one major continent, looking from the viewport now like an inverted pine tree. The effect of the whole was like Christmas wrapping paper with the colors reversed.

One more day, and she'd finally be there.

Sam stepped up behind her. "Beautiful, isn't it?"

"And how." She gazed at the planet in silence for a moment and then turned to Sam. "So how did Repnik think he would be able to gather data on the women's language without a female xenolinguist?"

"He wanted to plant more probes and use the technicians and crew of the *Penthesilea*."

She shook her head. "But they're not trained in working with an alien language."

"That's what Ainsworth said." He raised one eyebrow and smiled. "Except he added that they were needed on the ship for the jobs they'd been hired to do."

Toni chuckled despite the ache in her gut. "I think I'm going to be very grateful you're on this team, Sam."

Sam grinned. "Ditto."

[3]

F rom: *The Allied Interstellar Community General Catalog. Entry for Sgr 132-3, also known as Christmas, or Kailazh (land) in the native tongue.*

The third planet in the system of Sgr 132 is 1.2 AU from its sun, has a diameter of 15,840 kilometers, a density of 3.9, and 0.92G. The day is 16.7 standard hours and the year 743 days (1.42 Earth years). It is iron poor but rich in light metals. Satellites: three shepherd moons within a thin ring of debris. Land mass consists largely of one supercontinent covering most of one pole and extending south past the equator. It is now known to be a seeded planet of hominid inhabitants with a number of plants and animals also related to Terran species. Date of original colonization of the planet is as yet unknown. Technological status: pre-automation, primitive machines, rudimentary scientific knowledge. There is no written language.

[4]

The first thing Toni noticed when she stepped off the shuttle was the scent of the air, tantalizing and slightly spicy, as if someone were baking cookies with cardamom and cinnamon.

The second thing she noticed was the gravity. Christmas had slightly lower gravity than Earth, but Toni had grown up on Mars, and it certainly felt more like home than Admetos had. Her joints still ached from the large planet's crushing gravity. Thank God she had been transferred.

The rings were only the third thing she noticed. They arched across the southern sky like some kind of odd cloud formation, pale but still visible in the daylight.

Sam saw the direction of her gaze. "Wait until you see them at sunset."

Toni nodded, smiling. "I wanted to say I can imagine, but I'm not sure I can."

Irving Moshofski, the xenoteam geologist, stepped forward to introduce himself and shook Toni's hand. "Nice to meet you, Dr. Donato. Gates and Repnik are waiting for us in town."

They followed Moshofski to their ground transportation, an open carriage drawn by descendants of Terran horses, but taller and with lighter bone structure. This pair was a reddish-brown much deeper than the bays of Earth.

Toni took another deep breath of the air. "I swear, if they hadn't already named it Christmas for the colors, they would have changed the name to Christmas when they smelled the place."

"Everyone familiar with Terran Western culture says that," Moshofski said.

She climbed up into the open carriage behind Ainsworth and noted that it was well sprung, the workmanship of the wood smooth, and the leather seats soft. Their driver was a young Mejan man, tall and willowy, his skin a lovely copper color. As they settled into their seats, Toni greeted him in Alnar ag Ledar, "the language of the sea" — the universal language used by men and women on Christmas to communicate with each other.

Their driver lifted the back of his hand to his forehead in the Mejan gesture of greeting. "Sha bo sham, tajan."

She returned the gesture and turned to Ainsworth, suppressing a chuckle. "Why did he call me 'mother'?"

"That seems to be a term of respect for women here."

"At least that's something. But it looks like I still have a lot to learn."

Ainsworth nodded. "We all do. We strongly suspect the Mejan are withholding information from us. They're very reluctant to begin any kind of treaty negotiations with the Allied Interstellar Community."

"They don't trust us," Moshofski said.

Toni shrugged. "Is there any reason why they should?"

She leaned forward to address the driver, speaking rapidly in the men's language. "Moden varga esh zhamkaned med sherned?" *Do you trust the men from the sky?*

The driver looked over his shoulder at her and chuckled. "Roga desh varga an zhamnozhed, tajan." *Like I trust the stars.* Toni noticed that the laughing eyes in his copper-brown face were an extraordinary smoky green color.

She raised one eyebrow. "Moshulan sham beli?" *Not to fall on you?*

He laughed out loud, and Toni leaned back in her seat, grinning.

The landing base was about ten kilometers outside of the biggest town, Edaru, and she studied the landscape avidly during the trip. She loved the sights and scents and sounds of strange worlds, the rhythms of a new language, the shape and color of plants she had never seen before. For someone from Earth, the red hues of the landscape on Christmas might have conjured associations of barrenness, although the rich shades from magenta to burnt umber were from the native vegetation itself, the wide, strangely-shaped leaves of the low-growing plants and the fronds of the trees. But it never would have occurred to Toni to associate reds and umbers with barrenness. For someone from Neubrandenburg on Mars, red was the color of homesickness.

Toni didn't notice Edaru until they were practically upon it. They came over a rise and suddenly the city, crowded around a large bay, was spread out before them. The buildings were low and close to the water. Despite occasional flooding, the Mejan were happiest as close to the sea as possible.

At the sight of their vehicle, people came out of their houses, standing in doorways or leaning on windowsills to watch them pass. A number lifted the backs of their hands to their foreheads in the Mejan gesture of greeting.

Christmas was one of the half-dozen seeded planets in the known universe, and as on other such planets, the human population had made some physical adjustments for life in the given environment, most obviously in their height and the prominent flaps of skin between their fingers. But to Toni, who had spent two years now on Admetos among what the human members of AIRA often referred to as the giant ants, they didn't appear alien at all, or at least only pleasantly so. The people she saw were tall, light-boned, dark-skinned and wide-chested, with long hair in various hues which they wore interlaced with thin braids enhanced by colorful yarn. She was surprised at how little difference there was in the styles worn by the men and the women — not what she would have expected from a world where the women spoke a separate, "secret" language.

Ships and boats of various sizes were docked at the wharves, and one large ship was sailing into port as they arrived. The materials sent to her had described them as primitive craft, but she found them graceful and beautiful. The long, low stone houses had rows of windows facing the sea and were ornamented with patterns of circles and waves in shades of red and purple and green and blue on a background of yellow. Some larger houses were built in a u-shape around a central courtyard. Toni stared and smiled and waved. It looked clean and peaceful, the children content and the women walking alone with their heads held high.

The common house — the main government building of Edaru — was located in the center of town near the wharves. Councilor Lanrhel himself waited for them, the back of his hand touching his forehead in greeting. She couldn't help thinking it looked like he was shading his eyes to see them better.

Lanrhel was a handsome man, even taller than the average Mejan, with streaks of gray in his red-

dish-brown hair, the gray looking almost like an ex-
tra shade in the colors of his braids. The pale, tooled
leather of his short cape, the garment worn in the
warm half of the year, was the same length as his tu-
nic, reaching just past the tops of his thighs. He stood
in the doorway, his open palm in front of his forehead, and Toni returned the gesture as she approached the building. When Lanrhel didn't relax,
she glanced at Sam and Ainsworth, unsure what to
do. Perhaps she had not made the gesture correctly.
She repeated it and said in the best local dialect she
could manage, "Negi eden an elamed elu mazhu velazh Edaru. An rushen eden sham." Which meant
something like *I'm honored to be a guest in Edaru, thank
you.* Except that the language of the Mejan had no
verb for "to be" and tenses were expressed in auxiliary verbs which could go either before or after the
main verb, depending on the emphasis.

The councilor smiled widely and lowered his
arm, and Toni winced, realizing she had used the
male first person pronoun. Her first official sentence
on Christmas, and it was wrong. She was glad Repnik wasn't there. Sam and Ainsworth didn't seem to
notice that she'd made a mistake, but when she
glanced back at the driver with the smoky green eyes,

she saw that he too had a grin on his wide lips.

"We are happy to have you visit our city," Lanrhel said and led them into the common house. They crossed a central hallway and entered a large room where about a dozen people were seated in a circle in comfortable chairs and sofas. Low tables were scattered in the center, and on them stood strange-looking fruits in glossy bowls made of the shells of large, native beetles. Decorative lace hangings graced the walls.

Lanrhel announced them, and the others rose. Toni was surprised to see almost as many women as men, all garbed in soft, finely tooled leather of different colors. Leather was the material of choice of the Mejan, and their tanning methods were highly advanced. Sam had speculated it was because they lived so much with water, and leather was more water-resistant than woven materials.

She recognized Repnik immediately. She knew his face from photos and vids and holos. He was thin and wiry, with deep wrinkles next to his mouth and lining his forehead. Despite age treatments, the famous linguist looked old, used-up even, more so than the images she'd seen had led her to believe. He was also shorter than she expected, barely topping her eyebrows.

He came forward slowly to shake her hand. "Ms. Donato?" he said, omitting her title.

Two could play that game. "Mr. Repnik. I'm honored to be able to work with you."

His eyes narrowed briefly. "It really is unfortunate that you were called to Christmas unnecessarily. I'm sure you will soon see that there is little contribution for you to make here. Despite the sex barrier, I've managed to collect enough material on my own to be able to study and analyze the women's dialect." Sam had warned her on ship, but Repnik's unwelcoming attitude still stung. She did her best not to let it show, keeping her voice level. "A dialect? But it was my understanding that Alnar ag Eshmaled couldn't be understood by the men."

"Ms. Donato, surely you are aware that speakers of different dialects often cannot understand each other."

She bit her lip. If she was going to have a hand in deciphering the women's language, she had to get along with him. Instead of arguing, she shrugged and gave Repnik a forced smile. "Well, as they say, a language is a dialect with an army and a navy. And that's not what we have here, is it?"

Repnik gave her a pleased nod. "Precisely."

Jackson Gates, the team exobiologist, moved between them and introduced himself, earning Toni's gratitude. He was a soft-spoken, dark-skinned man with graying hair and beard, obviously the type who cared little about cosmetic age treatments. She judged his age at barely over fifty.

Lanrhel then introduced her to the other members of the Edaru council. The oldest woman, Anash, came forward and presented Toni with a strip of decorative lace, similar to the beautiful hangings on the walls. Toni lifted the back of her hand to her forehead again and thanked her.

The multitude of introductions completed, they sat down on the leather-covered chairs and couches, and Ainsworth asked in barely passable Mejan if anything had been decided regarding treaty negotiations with AIC. Lanrhel looked at Toni, and she repeated the request, adding the correct inclinations and stripping it of the captain's Anglicized word order. Why hadn't the councilor referred to Repnik? She'd been studying like a fiend for the last month, but surely his command of the language was better than hers.

Lanrhel leaned across the arm of his chair and

murmured something to Anash. Toni caught mention of the treaty again, and the words for language, house, and her own name. Anash looked across the circle at her and smiled. She returned the smile, despite the headache she could feel coming on. The first day on a new planet was always difficult, and this time she'd had conflict brewing with her boss even before she got off the shuttle. But next to Anash, another woman had pulled out her crocheting (a far cry from the stiff formality of the official functions she'd had to endure on Admetos), a man with eyes the color of the sea on Christmas had joked with her, and she still had a sunset to look forward to.

And no one was going to toss her into the ocean just yet. She hoped.

[5]

From: Preliminary Report on Alnar ag Ledar, primary language of Christmas. Compiled 29.09.157 (local AIC date) by Prof. Dr. Hartmut Repnik, h.c. Thaumos, Hino, Marat, and Polong, Allied Interstellar Research Association first contact team xenolinguist, Commander, Allied Interstellar Community Forces.

The language of the Mejan people of Christmas is purely oral with both inflecting and agglutinating characteristics. Tense information seems to be given exclusively in an inflected auxiliary which takes the place of helping verbs and modals while also providing information on the addressee of the sentence. Nouns are gendered, masculine and feminine, but with some interesting anomalies compared to known languages. Adjectives are non-existent. The descriptive function is fulfilled by verbs (e.g. jeraz, "the state of being green").

[6]

The arc of the rings lit up like lacework in the last rays of the setting sun, while the sky behind it showed through purple and orange and pink. Toni took a deep breath and blinked away the tears that had started in her eyes at the shock of beauty. Beside her, Sam was silent, too wise to disturb her enjoyment of the moment.

They were sitting on the veranda of the house AIRA had rented for her and any other women from the ship who had occasion to come planetside. Together they watched as the colors faded and the sky grew dark. The small moons accompanying the rings appeared, while the brilliant lace became a dark band, starting in the east and spreading up and over.

"Maybe that's why they seem to set such a high store by lace," Toni finally said when the spectacle was over.

Sam nodded. "I've thought of that too."

She took a sip of the tea, sweet and hot with a flavor that reminded her subtly of ginger, and leaned back in her chair, pulling her sweater tighter around her. The night grew cold quickly, even though it was early fall and Edaru was in the temperate zone.

"What have you learned about the role of women since you've been here?" Toni asked.

"Well, since they will only talk to the men of Edaru, it's a bit difficult finding out anything. But they don't live in harems, that's for sure."

"Harems" was Repnik's term for the houses of women, although the residents could come and go as they pleased and the houses were off-limits for men completely, as far as the first contact team could determine.

She laughed, briefly and without humor. "I wonder what bit him."

Sam was quiet so long, she turned to look at him. In the flickering light of the oil lamp, his face was shadowed, his expression thoughtful. They had a generator and solar batteries for electricity in Contact House One and Two, but they tried to keep use of their own technology to a minimum.

"I don't think he ever had a life," Sam finally said. "Most people are retired by the time they reach the age of one hundred. But look at Repnik — what would he retire to? His reputation spans the known universe, but it's all he's got. There's no prestige in hanging out on a vacation planet, and I doubt if he knows how to have fun."

His generous interpretation of Repnik's behavior made her feel vaguely guilty. "True. But I still get the feeling he's got something against women."

"Could be. I heard he went through a messy divorce a few years back — his ex-wife was spreading nasty rumors about him. I'm glad I'm not the woman working under him."

"Bad choice of words, Sam."

He smiled. "Guilty as charged."

Mejan "music" from a house down the hill drifted up to them, an odd swooshing sound without melody which reminded Toni of nothing so much as the water lapping the shore. Some native insects punctuated the rhythm with a "zish-zish, zish-zish" percussion, but there were no evening bird sounds. According to Jackson Gates, the only native life forms of the planet were aquatic, amphibian, reptilian or arthropod. There were no flying creatures on Christmas at all — and thus no word for "fly" in the Mejan language. Since the arrival of the xenoteam, the term "elugay velazh naished" (*move in the air*) had come into use.

It was impossible for contact to leave a culture the way it was before. Leaving native culture untouched was an article of belief with AIRA, but it was also a myth.

Toni finished her tea and put down her mug. "It's occurred to me that Repnik is perhaps being led astray by the fact that Christmas is a seeded planet. Most of the other languages he worked on were of non-human species."

"Led astray how?"

"Well, when they look so much like us, you expect them to be like us too. Language, social structures, the whole bit."

"It's a possibility. Just don't tell him that."

"I'll try. But I have a problem with authority, especially when it's wrong."

Sam chuckled. "I don't think Repnik is serious about the harems, though. It's just his idea of a joke."

"Yeah, but there are also some odd things about

the language which don't seem to go along with his analysis. Grammatical gender for example. Repnik refers to them as masculine and feminine, but they don't match up very well with biological sex. If he's right, then 'pirate' and even 'warrior' are both feminine nouns."

"I don't have any problem with that."

Toni pursed her lips, pretending to be offended. "But I do."

"I probably get them wrong all the time anyway."

"Don't you use your AI?" Like herself, Sam had a wrist unit. AI implants had been restricted decades ago because they led to such a high percentage of personality disorders.

He shrugged. "I don't always remember to consult it. Usually only when I don't know a word."

"And there's no guarantee the word will be in the dictionary yet or even that the AI will give you the right word for the context, even if it is."

"Exactly."

Toni gazed out at the night sky. Stars flickered above the horizon, but where the rings had been, the sky was black except for the shepherd moons. Below, the bay of Edaru was calm, the houses nestled close to the water, windows now lit by candlelight or oil lamps. She wondered where the green-eyed driver was, wondered what the Mejan executed people for, wondered if she would get a chance to work on the women's language.

She repressed the temptation to sigh and got up. "Come on, I'll walk you back to the contact house. I need to talk to Ainsworth before he returns to the ship."

[7]

The legend of the little lace-maker
Recorded 30.09.157 (local AIC date) by
Landra Saleh, sociologist, first contact team, SGR
132-3 (Christmas / Kailazh).

As long as she could remember, Zhaykair had only one dream — to become the greatest maker of lace the Mejan had ever known. All young girls are taught the basics of crocheting, but Zhaykair did not want to stop at that. She begged the women of her village to show her their techniques with knots, the patterns they created, and she quickly found the most talented lace-maker among them. Saymel did not belong to Zhaykair's house, but the families reached an agreement, and the little girl was allowed to learn from Saymel, although the job of Zhaykair's house was raising cattle.

But before she had seen nine summers (*note: approximately thirteen standard years — L.S.*), Zhaykair had learned all Saymel had to teach her. She begged her clan to allow her to go to the city of Edaru, where the greatest lace-makers of the Mejan lived. Her mothers and fathers did not want to send her away, but Saymel, who could best judge the talent of the young girl, persuaded them to inquire if the house of Mihkal would be willing to train her.

The elders sent a messenger to the Mihkal with samples of Zhaykair's work. They had feared being ridiculed for their presumption, but the messenger returned with an elder of the house of Mihkal to personally escort Zhaykair to the great city of Edaru.

Zhaykair soon learned all the Mihkal clan could teach her. Her lace was in such great demand, and there were so many who wanted to learn from her, that she could soon found her own house. Her works now grace the walls of all the greatest families of the Mejan.

[8]

"**If** Repnik refuses to allow you to work on the women's language, I'm not sure what I can do to help," Ainsworth said.

"Then why did you send for me?" Toni was only marginally aware of the cool night air against her skin as their open carriage headed for the AIC landing base. If she hadn't returned to the contact house with Sam, she would have missed Ainsworth completely. A deliberate move on his part, she suspected now.

"I thought I could bring him around," the Captain said now.

"Can't you order him?"

"I don't think that would be wise. With a little

diplomacy, you can still persuade him. In the long run, he will have to see that he needs you to collect more data."

Toni rubbed her temples. The headache she'd first felt coming on during the introductions in the common house had returned with a vengeance. "He'll probably try to use remote probes."

"He already has. But since none of us are allowed in the women's houses, they can't be placed properly. We've tried three close to entrances and have lost them all."

"What happened to them?"

"One was painted over, one was stepped on and one was swept from a windowsill and ended in the trash."

Despite everything, she had to smile to herself.

They pulled up next to the temporary landing base, and the light from the stars and the moons was replaced by aggressive artificial light. Ainsworth patted her knee in a grandfatherly way. "Chin up, Donato. Do your work and do it well, and Repnik will recognize that you can be of use to him. We'll get that unknown language deciphered, and you will be a part of it. That's what you want, isn't it?"

"Yes." Maybe everyone was right and she was

just overreacting to Repnik's reluctance to let her work on the women's language. It was certainly nothing new for AIRA researchers to feel threatened by others working in the same field and jealously defensive of their own area of expertise. Toni had seen it before, but that didn't mean she had to like it. Her first day on Christmas was not ending well.

At least she'd had the sunset.

The Captain got out of the carriage and waved at her as the driver turned it around and headed back into town.

When they were nearing the city again, Toni leaned forward, propping her arms on the leather-covered seat in front of her. The driver was the same one they'd had this morning. Strange that she'd been so fixated on Ainsworth and her own problems that she hadn't even noticed.

He glanced over his shoulder at her and smiled but said nothing.

Toni took the initiative. "Sha bo sham."

"Sha bo sham, tajan." The planes of his face were a mosaic of shadow and moonlight, beautiful and unfamiliar.

"Ona esh eden bonshani Toni rezh tajan, al?" *Me you call Toni not mother, yes?*

He laughed and shook his head in the gesture of affirmative, like a nod in Toni's native culture. "Bonlami desh an. Tay esh am eladesh bonshani Kislan." *Honored am I. And you me will call Kislan.*

She smiled and offered her hand as she would have in her own culture. He transferred the reins to one hand, then took her own hand gently and pressed it to his forehead. His skin was warm and dry. She couldn't see his smoky green eyes in the starlight, but she could imagine them. When he released her hand, she could have sworn it was with reluctance.

Perhaps the day was not ending so badly after all.

The women of Anash's family, the house of Ishel, were gentle but determined — they would not allow Toni to learn Alnar ag Eshmaled from them, "the language of the house," until she promised not to teach it to any men. Which of course was impossible. The point of research funded by AIRA was for it to be published and made accessible to everyone in the known galaxy. There were laws against restricting access to data on the basis of sex. Access to data could be restricted on the basis of security clearance perhaps, but not on the basis of sex.

"Bodesh fadani eshukan alnar ag eshmaled," Anash said, her expression sympathetic. *No man may speak the language of the house. Permission-particle-tense-marker-present for female addressee verb negative-marker-subject object*: with the mind of a linguist, Toni broke down the parts of the sentence, trying to figure out whether the women favored different sentence structures than the men.

So they weren't going to speak their language with her. She had spent her first two days setting up house and getting her bearings, and now that she finally had an appointment with some of the women of the planet, she learned that Repnik was right — she wouldn't be able to do the job she had come here to do.

But at least they had welcomed her into the women's house and were less careful with her than with the men of the contact team. With the camera in her AI, she had recorded Anash and Thuyene speaking in their own language several times. She felt a little bad about the duplicity — she'd never had to learn a language by stealth before — but if she was going to do the job she'd been hired for, she didn't have a choice. And when it came right down to it, AIRA never asked anyone's permission to send out the probes used in the first stages of deciphering a new language. Stealth always played a role.

But what a dilemma. The Allied Interstellar Research Association was required to make their knowledge of new worlds public. Not to mention that Toni would only be able to make her reputation as a xenolinguist if she could publish the results of her research. Perhaps they could work out some kind of compromise with AIRA that would make it possible for her to study the women's language anyway.

"May I still visit this house?" Toni asked in the men's language.

Anash smiled. "We are happy to welcome the woman from the sky. And perhaps you can teach us the language you speak, just as the men of the sky teach the men of the people."

"Why is it that you will speak with the men of Edaru and not with the men of the first contact team?"

The smile vanished from Anash's face. "They are offensive." In the Mejan language it was more like "exhibit a state of offensiveness," a verb used for descriptive purposes, but it was nonetheless different

LOOKING THROUGH LACE

from the verb "to offend," which connoted an indi-
vidual action.

"What have they done?" Toni asked.

The older woman's face seemed to close up.
"They speak before they are spoken to."

Was that all it was? The men of the contact team
had offended the Mejan sense of propriety? "So men
of a strange house may not speak to a woman without permission?"

"They may not. That intimacy is only granted
within families."

How simple it was after all: someone had merely
made the mistake of not asking the right questions.
She had read stories of contact teams that had suf-
fered similar misunderstandings from just such a
mistake. But how was anyone supposed to know
which questions to ask when dealing with an utterly
alien culture? It was no wonder the same mistakes
were made over and over again.

Besides, their team had the excuse of having lost
their sociologist early into the mission.

Toni rose and lifted the back of her hand to her
forehead. "I will come again tomorrow at the same
time, if that is convenient."

"I will send word."

Toni started to nod — and then caught herself and shook her head.

Visiting an unfamiliar world was exhausting business.

[9]

DG: *sci.lang.xeno.talk*
Subject: *We aren't redundant yet (was Why I do what I do)*
From: *A.Donato@aira.org*
Local AIC date: *21.10.157*

<insultingly uninformed garbage snipped>

Okay, I'll explain it again, even though I've been through this so many times on the DGs it makes my head spin.

No, we can't just analyze a couple of vids made by a drone and come up with a language. Even with all the sophisticated equipment for recording and analysis which we now possess, at some stage in deciphering an alien tongue we're still dependent on the old point and repeat method. The human element of interaction, of trial and error, remains a necessary part of xenolinguistics. IMNSHO, the main reason for this is that analyzing an alien language, figuring out the parts of speech and the rules at work (which is the really tough part, and *not* simple vocabulary), is more than just "deciphering" — a very unfortunate word choice, when it comes right down to it. "Deciphering" implies that language is like a code, that there is a one-to-one correspondence between words, a myth which supports the illusion that all you have to do is substitute one word for another to come up with meaning. Language imperialists are the worst sinners in this respect, folks with a native tongue with pretensions towards being a diplomatic language, like English, French or Xtoylegh.

People who have never learned a foreign language, who have always relied on the translation modules in their AIs to do a less-than-perfect job for them, often can't conceive how difficult this "deciphering" can be, with no dictionaries and no grammar books. An element you think at first is a noun could be a verb. Something interpreted as an indefinite article could very well be a case or time marking. You have no idea where the declensions go, no idea if the subject of the verb comes first or last or perhaps in the middle of the verb itself.

No linguistics AI ever built has been idiosyncratic enough to deal satisfactorily with the illogical aspects of language. Data analysis can tell you how often an element repeats itself and in which context, it can make educated guesses about what a particular linguistic element *might* mean, but the breakthroughs come from intuition and hunches.

AIs have been able to pass the Turing test for two centuries now, but they still can't pass the test of an unknown language.

[10]

As she left the women's house, Kislan was coming down the street in the direction of the docks.

"Sha bo sham, Kislan."

"Sha bo sham, Toni." He pronounced her name with a big grin and a curious emphasis on the second syllable. After three days planetside, she was beginning to see him with different eyes. She recognized now that the colors braided into his hair signified that by birth he was a member of the same family as Councilor Lanrhel himself, and he had "married" into the house of Ishel, one of the most important merchant clans in the city of Edaru. It seemed the council of Edaru had sent a very distinguished young man as transportation for their guests.

And he was part of some kind of big communal marriage.

"Where are you off to?" she asked in Mejan.

"The offices of Ishel near the wharves. A ship has returned after an attack by pirates and we must assess the damage."

"Are pirates a problem around here?"

Kislan shook his head in the affirmative. "It is especially bad in the east."

They stood in the street awkwardly for a moment, and then Kislan asked, "Where do you go now? May I walk with you?"

"Don't you have to get to work?"

He shrugged. That at least was the same gesture she was used to. "There is always time for conversation and company."

Toni grinned. "I'm on my way back to the contact house."

Kislan turned around and fell into step next to her. She asked him about his work and he asked her about hers, and it occurred to her how odd it was that this particular social interaction was so much

RUTH NESTVOLD

like what she had grown up with and seen on four planets now.

Talking and laughing, they arrived at the contact house in much less subjective time than it had taken Toni to get to the house of Anash — and it was uphill. After they said their goodbyes, she watched Kislan stride down to the wharves, starting to worry about her own peace of mind.

But when she entered the main office of the contact house, she had other things to worry about.

"I hope you will remember to remain professional, Donato," Repnik said.

Toni resisted the urge to retort sharply and leaned against the edge of a table. There were no AIRA regulations forbidding personnel from taking a walk with one of the natives — or even sleeping with one, as long as the laws of the planet were not broken.

She ignored the implied criticism. "Kislan was telling me about how they lost a ship to pirates. What do we know about these pirates?"

"Not much," Sam said. "Ainsworth wants to do some additional surveillance of the eastern coast."

"How did your meeting with Anash go?" Repnik asked.

She took a deep breath. "They won't speak their language with me until I promise no men will ever learn it."

Repnik shrugged. "I told you your presence here was unnecessary."

Didn't he even have any intellectual curiosity left, any desire to figure out the puzzle? Whether he resented her presence or not, if he still had a scientific bone left in his body he would be taking advantage of having her here.

She stood and began to pace. "Wouldn't it be possible to work out a deal with AIRA? Something that would allow us to reach an agreement with the women about their language? If Alnar ag Eshmaled had a special status, then only certain researchers would have access to the information."

"You mean, *women* researchers."

Toni stopped pacing. "Well, yes."

"Which would mean I, the head of this contact team, would be barred from working on the women's language."

She barely registered the minor victory of Repnik now referring to Alnar ag Eshmaled as a language. She had painted herself into a very hazardous corner. "I was only thinking of how we could keep from offending the women of of this planet."

"And how you could get all the credit for our findings."

"I didn't —"

Repnik stepped in front of her, his arms crossed in front of his chest. "I would suggest that you try to remember that you are an assistant in this team. Nothing more."

Toni didn't answer for a moment. Unfortunately, that wasn't the way she remembered the description of her assignment to Christmas. But it had named her "second" team xenolinguist. Which meant that if Repnik saw her as an assistant, she was an assistant, and there wasn't anything she could do about it. "Yes, sir. Anything else?"

"Tomorrow morning I would like you to work on compiling a more extensive dictionary with the material we have collected in the last several weeks."

"Certainly, sir." She picked her bag up off the floor and left Contact House One for the peace and safety of Contact House Two before she could say anything she would regret later.

How could she have been so stupid? In terms of her career, it would have been smarter to suggest using her visits to install surveillance devices, even if that would have been questionable within the framework of AIRA regulations. But of course Repnik would never agree to a strategy that would allow her to work on one of the languages of Kailazh exclusively.

When would she learn?

Toni pushed open the door of her house, slipped off her jacket and hung it over the back of a chair. Well, she was not about to break the laws of her host planet, Repnik or no Repnik, so before she hooked her mobile AI into her desk console, she set up a firewall to keep the men on the team from learning the women's language by accessing her notes.

Once her privacy was established, she told the unit to replay the women's conversation. The sounds of their voices echoed through the small house while she got herself something to eat.

"Index mark one," she said after the first short conversation was over, and her system skipped ahead to the next conversation. The first thing she noticed was that the women's language had a number of rounded vowel sounds which were absent in the men's, something like the German Umlaut or the Scandinavian "ø." At the same time, however, there were quite a few words which sounded familiar.

She finished the bread and cheese and tea and wiped her mouth on a napkin. "System, print a transcript of the replayed conversations using the spelling system developed by Repnik, and run a comparison with the material already collected on the men's language."

"Any desired emphasis?"

"Possible cognates, parallel grammatical structures, inflections."

While the computer worked, she laid out the printed sheet of paper on the desk in front of her. Sometimes she found it easier to work in hard copy than with a projection or on a screen. Doodling with a pencil or pen on paper between the lines could help her to see new connections, possibilities too far-fetched for the computer to take into consideration — but exactly what was needed for dealing with an arbitrary, illogical human system like language.

The transcript was little more than a jumble of letters. Before the initial analysis, the computer only added spaces at very obvious pauses between phonemes.

Pencil in hand, Toni gazed at the first two lines, the hodgepodge of consonants and vowels.

Tün shudithunföslodi larasethal segumshuyethun rhünem kasem alandaryk.

Athneshalathun rhün semehfarkari zhamdentakh.

The last recognized unit of meaning looked like a plural. Plural was formed in the men's language by adding the prefix "zham-" to the noun. There was no telling if those particular sounds were the same in the women's language, or even if the plural was built the same, but at least it gave her a place to start.

There was a faint warning beep, and the computer announced in its business-like male voice, "Initial analysis complete."

Toni looked up. "Give me the possible cognates. Output, screen." A series of word pairs replaced an image of the landscape of Neubrandenburg.

Dentakh - tendag.

But why would the women be discussing pirates in the middle of a conversation about languages? Was the cognate the computer had come up with correct? And if it was, what did it mean?

After she'd returned home from Contact House One, Toni had begun to feel another stress headache coming on — but now it had disappeared completely and without drugs.

She had a puzzle to solve.

"Print out the results of the analysis," she said, pulling her chair closer to the table holding the console.

Toni went to work with a smile.

[11]

From: *Preliminary Report on Alnar ag Eshmaled, secondary language of Kailazh (Christmas). Compiled 28.11.157 (local AIC date) by Dr. Antonia Donato, second xenolinguist, Allied Interstellar Research Association first contact team. (Draft)*

The men's and women's languages of Kailazh (Christmas) are obviously related. While this does not completely rule out an artificially constructed secret language, as has been observed in various cultures among classes wanting to maintain independence from a ruling class, the consistency in the phonetic differences between the cognates discovered so far seems to indicate a natural linguistic development. A further argument against a constructed language could be seen in sounds used in the women's language which are nonexistent in the men's language.

Interestingly enough, the women's language appears to have the more formal grammar of the two, with at least two additional cases for articles (dative and genitive?), as well as a third form for the second person singular, all of which are unknown in Alnar ag Ledar. To confirm this, however, much more material will need to be collected.

[12]

She'd had approximately three hours of sleep, when her mobile unit buzzed the next morning.

Toni burrowed out from under the pile of blankets and switched on audio. She didn't want anyone seeing her just yet.

"Yes?" she said and snuggled back into her warm nest of covers.

Repnik's voice drifted over to her, and she grimaced. "Donato, do you realize what time it is?"

"No. I still don't have the display set up," she replied, trying to keep the sleep out of her voice. "And I must have forgotten to set my unit to wake me last night. Sorry."

An impatient "hmpf" came from her system.

"Jump lag or no jump lag, I'd like you over here, now."

The connection ended abruptly. Toni pushed the covers back and got up, rubbing her eyes. Nights were simply too short on Christmas — especially for someone who had forgotten to go to bed until the sun started coming up.

Leather togs on and coffee downed, she was soon back at Contact House One, keying in and correcting terms in the preliminary version of the dictionary. After giving her his instructions, Repnik had left with Sam for a tour of the tannery outside of town, where they would ask questions and collect data and make discoveries. Like usual, Gates and Moshofski were already out looking at boulders and bushes and beasts.

While she was left with drudgery.

It was funny how something she had done regularly for the last five years now seemed so much more tedious than it ever had before. Toni loved words enough that even constructing the necessary databases had always held a certain fascination for her — on her previous jobs. Besides, it was a means to an end, a preliminary step on the ladder to becoming a first contact xenolinguist working on her own language.

Now it was a step down.

She spent the morning checking and correcting new dictionary entries that the automatic analysis had made, consulting the central AI on her decisions, and creating links to grammatical variations, as well as audio and visual files, where available. And all that on only three hours of sleep.

"Fashar," the computer announced. "Lace, the lace. Feminine. Irregular noun. Indefinite form fasharu."

Toni did a search for "rodela," another word for lace in the Mejan language, and then added links between the words. Under the entry "fashar," she keyed in, "See also 'rodela' (lace) and 'rodeli' (to create lace or crochet)." She would have to ask Anash what precisely the difference was between "rodela" and "fashar," if any — as yet, nothing was noted in their materials.

Outside the door of the lab, she heard the sound of voices. Sam and Repnik returning from field work. Having fun.

"Fashela," the computer announced. "Celebrate. Verb, regular."

"That's the attitude," Toni muttered.

The door opened, and Repnik entered, followed by Sam, who looked a little sheepish. Getting chummy with the top of the totem pole.

Repnik sauntered over to her desk. "How is our dictionary coming along?" he asked in that perky voice bosses had when they were happy in the knowledge that they were surrounded by slaves. And were particularly pleased in the status of the slave before them.

"I'm up to the 'f's now in checking entries and adding cross references. Our material is a little thin on specific definitions, though."

The faint smile on his face thinned out and disappeared. "It is, is it?"

He looked offended for some reason. Toni had only been pointing out a minor weakness, common in early linguistic analysis of new languages, certainly not something to get irritated about. Man, was he touchy. She would have to tread even more carefully.

She drew a deep breath. "I've been tagging synonyms where we don't have any contextual information. We need to know more about the kinds of situations where one word or the other would be most appropriate. Would you like to ask the Mejan about the synonyms, or should I?"

"Make a note of it," Repnik said shortly.

"Certainly, sir."

"I have another meeting with Councilor Lanrhel. I'll see you both again tomorrow."

"But —"

"Tomorrow, Donato."

When he was gone, Toni joined Sam next to the small holo well set up in the lab, where he was viewing a scene of what looked like a festival.

She touched his elbow. "I learned something the other day in the women's house that you might find interesting."

"Bookmark and quit," Sam said to the holo projector before he swiveled around on his chair to face her. "That's right, I wanted to ask you about that meeting, but you left pretty abruptly yesterday."

Toni pulled over a chair and straddled it, leaning her forearms on the back. "I know. I should have stuck around, but our boss is really getting to me. Maybe I'm overreacting, but I'm starting to get the feeling that Repnik wants to make me quit."

Sam shook his head. "You *are* overreacting. Your suggestion yesterday, logical as it was, was practically calculated to make him feel threatened. Just give him some time to get used to you."

"I'll try."

"So, what did you find out for me?"

Toni chuckled. "Right. Anash told me yesterday that there's no specific taboo on women speaking with strange men. The reason they won't speak with the men of our team is because they offend them by speaking before they are spoken to."

Sam's eyes lit up. "Really?"

She nodded. "Do you know if you're guilty of offensive behavior yet?"

"I don't think so. When I got here, Repnik told me there was a taboo against strangers speaking with Mejan women *at all*, so I didn't even try. Wow. This changes everything."

"Yup. I wanted to get together with Anash and Thuyene again this afternoon. Since you're not one of the offensive ones, I could ask if we could meet outside of the women's house sometime, at a neutral location where you could join us."

"That would be great if you could organize it!" Sam said, his dark eyes alight with enthusiasm. "But maybe you can find out first how I *am* supposed to conduct myself."

"The young one with the hair of night and eyes like a *likish*?" Anash asked. A likish was one of the native amphibian creatures of Kailazh, with both legs and fins and a nostril/gill arrangement on its back which reminded Toni vaguely of whales. She had yet to see a likish, but she had seen pictures, and she could appreciate the simile.

Not having adjectives, Alnar ag Ledar could be quite colorful, if the speaker chose some other way to describe something than using the attribute verbs.

"*Al*," Toni said. *Yes.*

Anash gazed at her with a speculative expression — or at least what looked like it to Toni. Anash's eyes were slightly narrowed, her head tilted to one side, and her lips one step away from being pursed. "That one has not himself offended any of the women of Edaru," the older woman finally said. "You say he is a specialist in understanding the ways of a people?"

"Yes. He has replaced Landra Saleh, who I believe you met before she became ill."

"Then we will meet with him two days from now in the common house."

That would mean Toni would temporarily have to give up her surreptitious recordings in the women's house — but helping Sam would be worth it.

And when she told Sam the women had agreed to meet with him, his reaction more than made up for it. He was so enthusiastic, she felt as if she'd given him a present.

The day of their appointment, they walked together down the hill to the center of town, Toni sporting a new leather cape she'd purchased for a couple of ingots of iron from the string she wore around her neck. Iron was much more precious on Kailazh than gold.

As they wandered through the streets of the city, she examined the stands they passed. Most of the vendors they saw were men, but occasionally a lone woman sat next to bins of fruits and vegetables or shelves of polished plates and bowls made from the shells of oversized bugs. Such a female vendor would have to deal with male customers alone, some of whom would necessarily be strangers. Toni wondered what the protocols for such transactions might be. Perhaps now that they had started asking the right questions, they could discover something more about the rules governing relations between the sexes on Kailazh.

She did her best to act naturally on this alien world, but often she felt like a circus animal. People peered out of their windows at them as they passed, and children ran up to them, giggling and pointing and staring, or hid behind their mothers' or fathers' legs. It hadn't been any different on Admetos, but the beings staring after her there had looked like ants. As a result, it had been easier for her to ignore their behavior. But these were *people,* at least in a more visceral way for Toni, since she was a hominid herself.

It would take some time getting used to.

"From what you've learned since you arrived, do you know when one of those ceremonial gifts of lace is appropriate?" Toni asked Sam.

"No. But it seems to be something only given by women. We aren't on sure enough ground yet to start messing with symbolic gestures."

Toni gave a playful snort of disgust. "You've already been here two weeks! What have you been doing in all that time?"

Sam chuckled. "I may not trust myself with symbols, but I'm pretty sure we could bring Anash a bottle of that lovely dessert wine that Edaru is famous for. Have you tried it yet?"

"I'm still trying to stick mostly to foods I'm familiar with. I don't want to end up offworld like your predecessor."

"Well, once you feel daring enough, take my word for it, it's an experience you don't want to miss. And according to Jackson, the fruit *kithiu* which they use to make *denzhar* is descended from plain old Terran grapes."

"Okay, you've convinced me. Where's the nearest wine dealer?"

The merchant was a man, so Toni didn't have a chance to see what the interaction would be between Sam and a female merchant. They paid with a small bead each from the strings of precious metals they wore around their necks, and arrived at the common house just as Kislan was helping Anash and Thuyene out of an open carriage.

To her surprise, Toni felt a pang of something resembling jealousy. These two women both belonged to Kislan's family, and while Anash was probably old enough to be his mother, Thuyene wasn't much more than Toni's age; probably less biologically on this world without age treatments. Her glossy reddish-brown hair hung in a single thick braid to her waist, laced with threads the colors of her birth clan and her chosen clan. Her amber eyes were full of life and intelligence. And Kislan was in some kind of group marriage arrangement with her. Did he hold her hand a little longer than that of Anash? Or was her feverish, human-male-deprived imagination just taking her for a ride?

Anash waved. Toni gave herself an inner shake and returned the gesture.

"I am glad you did not have to wait," Anash said. "I was afraid business went longer than expected." She looked at Sam curiously, but he said nothing, just lifting the back of his hand to his forehead in the gesture of greeting.

Kislan said something rapidly to the women of his family in a low voice that Toni couldn't understand. She looked away, hoping her face wasn't as flushed as she felt.

The room Anash led them to in the common house was smaller than the one where they had met on Toni's arrival, but it was a comfortable, sunny room with large windows facing a central courtyard and lace hangings decorating the walls.

"My colleague Samuel Wu has brought you a gift

in hopes that relations between you might begin in a spirit of harmony and trust," Toni said in the Mejan language as they took seats on upholstered brocade sofas. This was the first time on Christmas she'd seen furniture covered in anything besides leather, and she wondered if this room was usually reserved for special occasions.

Kislan sat down beside her, and Toni felt her pulse quicken and her cheeks grow hot. She really had been living too long among ants.

Anash addressed Sam directly. "Sha bo sham, Samuel. We thank you, both for the thoughtful gesture and the respect that goes with it. We will be happy to tell you of Mejan ways. We too are curious to hear about the ways of the people of the stars."

Sam got the bottle of *denzhar* out of his bag, while Toni checked the AI at her wrist to make sure she'd set it for record mode. Across from her, Thuyene pulled a crocheting project out of her own bag, and Toni suppressed a smile.

"Sha bo sham, tajan," Sam said, leaning across the table and presenting the wine to Anash. "I am honored to be able to speak with you and hope that my gift is welcome."

It appeared they had chosen well. A pleased

smile touched Anash's lips as she accepted the bottle, and Toni almost sighed in relief.

Sam began by asking about the specific rules governing interaction between men and women. They soon learned that in addition to the disrespect shown if a man not of a woman's family spoke before being spoken to, there was a whole battery of taboos concerning what was appropriate when and with whom and at what age. It reminded Toni vaguely of what she had read long ago about Victorian England — except for the group marriages, of course.

While the conversation was fascinating, at least as far as Toni understood it, they never came anywhere near to the topic of sex proper, and the group marriages practiced on Christmas in particular. Sam was obviously doing his best to tread carefully, and open discussion of sexual practices was taboo in the majority of cultures in the galaxy.

"Boys move into the house of men when they are weaned, correct?" Sam asked.

Anash shook her head in the affirmative. "Yes." Toni felt the heat from Kislan's body next to her.

"Is there any kind of ritual associated with the move?"

"To leave the mother is to leave the sea, so there

is a celebration on the beach called *mairheltan*."

Kislan spoke up. "It is the first memory I have, the *mairheltan*."

"What does the ritual consist of?" Sam asked.

"The boy who is to leave the house of women goes into the water with the mother and comes back out by himself," Thuyene explained. "Then there is a feast with fish and *dashik*, and the child receives a leather cape and a length of lace."

She used the term "roda ag *fashar*" not "rodel" when she spoke of lace. Toni remembered the dictionary entries she'd been working on the other day and couldn't help asking an off-topic question. "What exactly is the difference between 'fashar' and 'rodel'?"

Thuyene lifted up the crocheting she was working on. "This is 'rodela.'" She pointed to a wall hanging just past Kislan's shoulder. "This is 'fashar.'"

It was all lace to Toni, but she was beginning to see the difference. "So 'fashar' is the piece when it is finished?"

"Not always. The 'fashar' given to a boy when he joins the house of men only begins. The women of his house can add to the 'fashar' he is given as a boy."

Toni would have liked to find out more about

the words, but Sam was asking another question himself. "If a boy has already begun to talk before he leaves the house of women, how is it he doesn't learn to speak the women's language?"

Anash chuckled. "His mother corrects him if he speaks the language that is wrong."

Sam laughed and looked at Kislan, who smiled and shrugged. Toni could see how that would be a very effective method to keep boys from learning the women's language.

The meeting continued until the light through the windows began to grow dim, and ended with a promise to show Sam around town the next day to see some of the places where women worked in Edaru. Anash couldn't accompany him herself, but she would see to it that one of the women of her house met him tomorrow morning at the Mejan equivalent of a café in the main square. Of course, he still was not allowed to visit any of the houses of women, but his enthusiasm at the sudden progress in his research was obvious in his voice and posture.

Toni had learned quite a bit herself that afternoon. It was surprising what you could discover if you only knew which questions to ask. Anash and Thuyene had been astonished at some of the things they told them about their native cultures as well, in particular the institution of marriage, which they only seemed to be able to understand in terms of property, of one partner "belonging" to the other.

She'd done her best to suppress her awareness of Kislan beside her, but the discussion of different forms of partnership unfortunately had quite the opposite effect. As a human male of Kailazh, Kislan was both familiar and exotic at the same time. A very desirable male, especially after she had spent all too long on a world full mostly of giant ants. All the senses in her body were screaming "potential partner" for some primordial reason, and she had the uncomfortable sensation that Kislan was aware of her in a similar way — even though he was part of some kind of group marriage with the women across from her.

He didn't speak much, and neither did she. Instead, they sat there, the lovely view of the red fern and coral-like vegetation visible through the window across from them.

On one level, Toni was relieved when Anash called an end to the meeting. On another, she wished they could continue to sit there and talk for hours, learn more about social arrangements on Christmas, find out how the Mejan viewed their own history. And on the primal level, she was humming. Feeling that kind of physical attraction again after so long, almost knee to knee and elbow to elbow, was mind- and body-racking.

She barely looked at Kislan as they took their leave, mentally kicking herself for the way she was responding to his physical presence.

"Their reaction to marriage forms in Terran culture was interesting, don't you think?" Sam said when they were out of earshot of the common house.

"You mean in terms of property?" Toni asked.

"Exactly. I wish we could find out more about their history. It makes me wonder if slavery might not be too far removed in the Mejan consciousness. Oh, and thank you."

"What for?"

Sam smiled that slow smile she had learned to like so much from the vids they had sent each other. "For giving me a crack at half a society."

[13]

The Legend of the Three Moon

Once, in the early days of the Mejan, after the Great War, there was a very attractive young man, more handsome than any other in all of the thirteen cities. When he came of age, Zhaykair, mother of the house of Sheli, asked if he would join their family, and he came willingly. The house had a good reputation for the fine lace it produced, and the women of the house were beautiful, their necks long, their shoulders wide, and their skin glossy.

A sister of the house looked on the man with desire and wished to have him for herself alone. The husband saw her beauty, her hair the color of night and her eyes like a dashik flower, and he swore to do anything for her; she made his blood run hotter than any woman he had ever seen. The sister went mad at the thought of him lying with other women, and she made him promise he would resist all others for her sake.

Zhaykair saw what her sister was doing and how it poisoned the atmosphere in the house. She went to the councilor to ask what he thought should be done with the young man.

"We will bring them before us and ask them what is more important, the peace of the house or their love."

So the sister and the husband were brought before the council. The mother gazed at the sister with sadness and said, "I cannot believe that you would disturb the peace of the house this way."

The sister began to cry. The husband jumped up, his hand raised against Zhaykair. When the sister saw what he intended to do, she threw herself upon him, but not before he had struck the mother.

By law, the husband had to be given back to the sea for striking a mother. The sister refused to let him go alone, and they returned to the sea together.

Zhaykair could not bear the thought of what had happened in her house and the sister's betrayal, and she followed them soon after. The sea in her wisdom wanted to make a lesson of them and gave the three lovers to the sky.

And now the sister, who never wanted to share the young man with another, must share him with Zhaykair every night. Sometimes it is the sister who is closer and sometimes the mother, but only for a short time does the sister ever have him to herself.

[14]

The next day, Toni met with the women on their own turf again. She was shown into the central courtyard by a beautiful young woman wearing the colors of Ishel and Railiu in the dark braids scattered through her heavy hair. The air was crisp and the sun bright, and they wandered among the houses, Anash and Thuyene pointing out more of the complex.

The first contact team referred to the residences of the families of Edaru as "houses" for the sake of simplicity — in actuality, they consisted of several buildings, with the young girls living in one, the mothers of the youngest children with their babies and toddlers in another, and the grown women with no children below the age of about three standard years in a third. There was also a smaller version of the Edaru common house, with a family refectory and rooms where all could gather and talk, play games, tell stories. Perhaps on the surface the setup did resemble a harem, but it obviously wasn't one.

"I hope you did not lose much in the pirate attack," Toni said during a lull in the conversation.

Anash looked grim. "Too much."

"This is the second ship attacked this summer," Thuyene added.

Suddenly, Toni realized how she might be able to get the Mejan to agree to the AIC treaty. Anash was obviously one of Lanrhel's main advisers, and he would listen to what she had to say. "So you also have a problem with pirates," she said casually.

"Why do you say 'also'?" Anash asked.

"There are many pirates among the stars too. That is the purpose of the Allied Interstellar Community — to form a common defense against the pirates of the sky."

Of course, that wasn't the only purpose: interstellar trade and research were at least equally important, with the emphasis on "trade." But Toni doubted she could interest anyone on Kailazh in trade with distant points of light that figured prominently in stories told in the evening to pass the time.

"But why should we fear them?" Thuyene asked. "We do not travel the stars, so they cannot attack the ships of the people."

"It's not that easy," Toni said, suppressing thoughts of how the other woman might be spending her nights — in the Ishel main house with Kislan. "They might come here."

Anash started. "Attack Edaru? From the sky?"

"Certainly from the sky."

In their surprise, Anash and Thuyene didn't think to lower their voices when they began discussing rapidly in the women's language, and Toni was able to capture a lengthy conversation on her wrist unit.

Finally they turned back to her. "How can that be?"

"As soon as Kailazh was discovered, the news of another culture was known to all the worlds with access to the network of the Allied Interstellar Community." But, of course, the word she used in the Mejan language wasn't actually "network": the term the first contact team used to approximate the interstellar exchange of information referred to the trade of professional couriers who traveled between the thirteen cities, dispensing messages and news.

"I see," Anash said. "And in this way, we become a part of this community before we even give permission." She used some kind of qualifier for "permission" which Toni was unfamiliar with, but she didn't deem it the right time to ask what it meant. Anash lifted the back of her hand to her forehead, and Toni's heart sank — she was being dismissed.

"Thuyene will see you out of the house," Anash said and turned on her heel.

Together they watched her stride back to the central building. "You should have told us sooner," Thuyene said quietly.

"I didn't know it was so important."

"I believe you. There is much we still do not know about each other."

That was certainly true.

When she returned to Contact House One, Toni found Sam sitting tensely in his desk chair and Repnik standing next to him, his arms folded in front of his chest.

Repnik turned, not relaxing his defensive posture. The stress lines between his eyes were even more pronounced than usual and his face was pale. "I'm glad you have finally arrived, Donato. I hear you took Sam to meet with the women yesterday without my authorization."

Toni blinked. Sam didn't *need* Repnik's authorization. Certainly, Repnik had seniority, but the experts of a first contact team were free to pursue their research however they saw fit. *She*, by contrast, was only second linguist, so it was a bit more logical for Repnik to boss her around.

"Uh, yes."

"I won't have it. I've already told Sam that he is not to meet with the women again unless I arrange it."

Which meant never. The women refused to negotiate with Repnik, that much was clear.

She looked at Sam, his lips pressed together and misery in his eyes.

Toni at least didn't have much to lose. She could put her neck out where Sam obviously wasn't willing to. "But he's chief sociologist."

"And I'm head of the first contact team."

She couldn't believe it. Either he was so fixated

on maintaining complete control of the mission that he had lost it — or there was something he didn't want them to find out. She looked him in the eye, her hands on her hips. "Maybe we should see what Ainsworth has to say about that. Computer, open a channel to the *Penthesilea.*"

"Access denied."

"What?!"

"Access denied," the computer repeated, logical as always.

"Why?"

"Prof. Dr. Hartmut Repnik has restricted access to communications channels. I am no longer authorized to initiate off-site communications without his permission."

The completely mundane thought darted through Toni's mind that she would no longer be able to participate in the AIC discussion groups. As if that mattered right now.

"I don't want you visiting any of the houses of women without my approval, either," Repnik continued, addressing Toni.

"But we're here to learn about these people."

"And the two of you have been conducting unauthorized research. Now if you'll excuse me, I have

AIRA business to attend to."

When Repnik was out of the door, Toni turned to Sam. "Unauthorized research?"

Sam shrugged, looking wretched.

Toni dropped into the chair next to him. "So, you still think I'm overreacting?"

Sam didn't respond to her attempt at a joke. "We're stuck, you know. He's going to tell Ainsworth some story about us now."

She propped her chin in her hand. "You must have done something to set him off. Can you think what it might be?"

He shook his head. "I just told him about the meeting with Anash and Thuyene yesterday."

"So he doesn't want either of us speaking directly with the women. But why?"

Sam shook his head, and Toni got up and began to pace. "Look, Sam, he can't get away with this. If Repnik really does contact Ainsworth about us with some fairy tale, then we'll also have our say, and it should be obvious that he's giving orders that hinder the mission."

"And what if he lies?"

"We have to tell Gates and Moshofski what's up."

"They won't be in until tonight."

They stared at each other in silence for a moment. "I think I need to take a walk."

Sam gave her a weak smile and waved her out the door. "Go. I'll hold down the fort."

Toni walked, long strides that ate up the stone-paved streets. She had devoted most of her adult life to AIRA, and she didn't know what she would do if they threw her out. Given the number of interstellar languages she could speak, there would always be jobs for her, but if she went into translating or interpreting, she would no longer be involved in the aspect of language she enjoyed most, the puzzle of an unknown discourse.

At least she wouldn't have to work with any more ants.

The weather was turning, appropriate to her mood, the gray-green sky heavy with the threat of rain. Toni made her way through narrow side streets to the sea wall at the south end of town. The green ocean below crashed against the wall, sending shots of spray up to the railing where she stood, and the wind tangled her hair around her face. She pulled her leather cape tighter around her body and gazed out to sea. The lacy rings of sunset probably would not be visible tonight, blocked out by the coming storm.

She heard a footstep behind her and turned. Kislan. He gazed at her with eyes that matched the sea, and she realized she had come out here close to the docks hoping they might run into each other.

He raised the back of his hand to his forehead, and she returned the gesture. "Sha bo sham, Kislan."

"Sha bo sham, Toni."

Her name in his language sounded slower, more formal, less messy, the "o" rounded and full, the syllables distinct and clear. She wondered what "Antonia" would sound like on his lips. She'd never liked the name, but she thought she might if he said it.

"How do you greet a friend in your language, someone you are close to?" Toni asked.

"Sha bo foda," he said. "Dum gozhung 'sha.'" *Or simply "sha."*

"Can we use 'fo' and 'foda' with each other?" she asked, offering her hand in the gesture of her home-world.

He nodded, the negative on Kailazh, ignoring her hand. He didn't want to use the informal "you" form with her. He wouldn't take her hand anymore either, although he took Thuyene's when he was only leaving for an afternoon. But then, Thuyene was one of his wives, and she most certainly was not. She leaned her hip on the railing, gazing at the gray-green sea below the dark gray sky. There was no reason to feel hurt and every reason to feel relief. He was a part of the Ishel family, and she still didn't understand the way loyalty was regarded in these complex relationship webs. Definitely not something to get messed up with.

Tears began to collect at the corners of her eyes, and she wiped them away angrily. To her surprise, Kislan turned her to him and took her chin in one hand.

"Tell me," he said. The Mejan very rarely used the command form, and there was something shocking about it. It startled Toni into more honesty than she had intended.

"This is all so difficult."

He shook his head slowly and she gave a humorless laugh. Then her intellectual knowledge managed to seep through her emotional reaction. He *wasn't* disagreeing with her.

She twisted her face out of his hand and turned

around to grip the railing at the top of the sea wall. A pair of arms encased in soft leather came around her and a pair of hands with their strange, wonderful webbing settled on hers. "You don't understand. It is not allowed for us to speak so with each other."

His chest was wide and hard against her back, welcome and strong. She had the unrelated, illogical thought that he probably had the high lung capacity of most of the Mejan, and wondered how long he could stay underwater comfortably.

"Al," Toni said, *yes*, unsure what exactly she was saying "yes" to.

Then there were a pair of lips, soft and warm, against the back of her neck, and it was too late to consider anything. She was in way over her head, infatuated with a man who had about a dozen official lovers.

His arm moved around her shoulders and he steered her away from the railing along the sea wall, away from the city. "It hurts me to see you weep. I would keep you from being alone."

To their left, the stone walls of the nearest buildings were painted in bright colors, colors to make the heart glad, shades of yellow and red and sea green.

She pulled herself together and dried her cheeks

with the back of her hand. "It's no good. We barely understand each other."

"You speak our language very well."

"It's more than that. Our ways differ so much, when you say one thing, I understand another. We can't help but see each other through the patterns we know from the cultures we grew up with. Like looking through lace — the view isn't clear, the patterns get in the way."

Kislan shook his head — affirmation, she reminded herself. "Yes, I see. But I would never hurt you, Toni."

"Ah, but you do. I know it's not deliberate, but just by being a man who lives by the rules of the Mejan, you hurt me."

He shook his head again. "It has to do with the relationship between men and women in the culture where you come from?"

"Yes." Toni didn't trust herself with gestures.

They had nearly reached the end of the sea wall, and there were no buildings here anymore. Kislan took her hand in his own webbed one.

"You would want to have me for yourself?" Kislan asked. "Like the sister in the legend of how the moons got into the sky?"

"It is the way things are done in the world I come from," Toni said defensively.

He smiled at her. "That is a story that lives in my heart."

She stopped, surprised. "I thought it was meant to show the People how *not* to behave, a lesson."

Kislan laughed out loud. "Have you no stories in your culture that are meant to teach but tempt instead?"

Of course they did. Human nature was stubborn and contrary, and no matter what the culture, there would always be those who would rebel, who would see something different in the stories than what was intended. Even in a relatively peaceful, conformist society like that of the Mejan.

"Yes, there are some similarities."

They leaned against the railing and looked out at the harbor of Edaru, at the graceful, "primitive" ships swaying with the waves. The sea was unquiet, the sky still heavy.

Kislan let his shoulder rest against hers. "Although I know nothing about the worlds on the stars, I can understand a little how you cannot always make sense of our way of doing things. The People live all along the coast here, and the rule of the house is the same for all. But the pirates beyond the waters of the world and on the islands to the east live by rules hard for us to understand."

"What rules do they live by?"

"They have no houses and no loyalty. They buy and sell not only goods but also *zhamgodenta*."

That was a term Toni had not yet heard. "What does 'godenta' mean?"

"That is a word for a person who is bought and sold."

Slavery. Sam had been right.

[15]

From: *Mejan creation myth*
Recorded 01.10.157 (local AIC date) by Landra Saleh, sociologist, first contact team, SGR 132-3 (Christmas / Kailazh).

The war between the Kishudiu and the Tusalis lasted so many years and cost so many lives, there were no longer any women alive who had not known a life without war. Soon there were no longer any men left at all.

The women of the Kishudiu and the Tusalis looked around them at the destruction of their homes, saw that there was nothing left to save and no enemies left to fight. Together, they took the last ships and fled by sea.

After sailing for almost as many days as the war had years, they came to a beautiful bay on the other side of the world, a haven of peace, a jewel. Edaru.

[16]

Jackson Gates and Irving Moshofski were already there when Toni returned to Contact House One. Two pairs of dark eyes and one pair of gray turned to her in unison when she entered the lab.

"This is unprecedented," Jackson said.

"I hope so," Toni said. "But since this is the only first contact team I've ever been on, my experience is a bit limited."

The men smiled, and the atmosphere became a shade less heavy.

"One of us will have to be here in the lab at all times in case the *Penthesilea* makes contact," Moshofski said. "I checked the systems, and there doesn't seem to be a way for any of us to override Repnik's commands."

"So we have to wait until Ainsworth can do it," Toni said.

The other three nodded.

"I was beginning to wonder what Repnik was up to," Jackson said quietly. "He made a point of telling me you were having an affair with the young man who acted as your chauffeur from the landing base."

Toni swallowed. "I — no — I'm attracted to him, but, I — no." Then through her embarrassment she picked up on a detail of what he had said. "You mean Kislan wasn't your chauffeur when you first arrived?"

"No. We had a much older man driving us."

"Hm. Was he also a member of the ruling clans?"

"I don't remember offhand the colors he wore in his hair, but I don't think so."

"Interesting." So why had they sent her Kislan?

There was little else they could do without being able to contact the *Penthesilea*, so they said goodnight to each other and sought out their separate quarters.

With all of the day's upheavals, Toni had almost

forgotten the recording she'd made in the morning, and she returned to the work she loved, relieved that she had something to take her mind off Repnik's irrational behavior.

The conversations she'd caught were a goldmine — or an iron mine, from the Mejan point of view. And it wasn't just the long exchange between Thuyene and Anash or the snippets from the other women in the Ishel family. The discoveries started when she began to study the unknown qualifier Anash had used when speaking to her. After analyzing the recordings of the women's language for similar occurrences of "kasem," she was almost certain it was a possessive pronoun.

Both the possessive and the genitive were unknown in the men's language — the linguistic forms for ownership.

Toni leaned back in her chair and regarded the notes she'd made in hard copy, the circles and question marks and lines and arrows. So what did she have? She had phonetic differences which seemed to indicate that the men's language had evolved out of the women's language and not the other way around. She had a gendered language in which the genders of the nouns didn't match up with gendered forms of address. She had warriors being named in one breath with pirates and pirates being named in one breath with language. She had a language spoken by men and named after the sea — and the sea was associated with the mother. She had grammatical cases that didn't exist in the men's language, a pairing which normally would lead her to conclude that the "secondary language" was the formalized, written language. If you looked at Vulgar Latin and Italian or any other of the common spoken languages in the European Middle Ages on Earth, it was the written language which had maintained the wealth of cases, while the romance languages which evolved out of it dispensed with much of that.

But the Mejan had no written language, because they had no system of writing.

She also had a boss who was doing his utmost to keep them from learning too much about the culture of the women.

And she had a man with eyes the color of a stormy green sea. A man who was married to about a dozen women at once.

Most of what she had were complications and questions. Where were the answers?

The next morning, Toni found Kislan on the docks, speaking with a captain of one of the ships belonging to his family. It probably would have been more logical to seek out Anash, but Toni didn't feel very logical.

Besides, her boss had pretty much forbidden her from speaking with the women of Christmas without his permission. Which she suspected meant never.

When he saw her striding his way, Kislan's eyes lit up, and her gut tightened in response. She touched her forehead with the back of her hand. "Sha bo dam," she said, using the plural second person. "I hope I'm not interrupting anything?"

Kislan nodded denial. "We are expecting a shipment of leather goods, and I merely wanted to see if it had arrived." He introduced Toni to the captain, Zhoran. She noted the threads braided into his hair, saw that he too wore the colors of both Lanrhel's family and the Ishel, and she looked at him more closely. His coloring was lighter than Kislan's, and he was obviously older, his golden-brown hair showing the first signs of gray at the temples. The bone structure of his face was very similar, though. She wondered if they were brothers.

Toni touched Kislan's elbow briefly. "May I speak with you alone?"

He shook his head. "Let us go to the office."

Toni followed him a short distance down a street leading away from the docks — away from the busy, noisy scene, much like that of any center for trade and travel. Despite the presence of horses and carriages, despite the color of the vegetation on the hills and the scent of the air, it reminded her a little of the many transit stations between wormhole tunnels that she had passed through on her travels between worlds. It looked nothing alike, but there was an energy level, an atmosphere, which was much the same, despite the different details.

Kislan had a small office in the rambling administration building of his family's trading business. On a table in the center of the room stood a counting machine similar to an abacus, and against one wall was a heavy door with a lock, the first lock Toni had even seen on Kailazh. But no desk. Without any system of writing, there was apparently no need for a desk.

When the door was closed behind her, Kislan

pulled her into his arms and held her tightly. "Time has crawled by since you left me yesterday," he murmured into to her hair.

The words and the arms felt incredibly good, but Toni couldn't allow herself to get involved with him — especially when she still didn't know whether fooling around outside the house was a sin or not. To judge by the legends she was familiar with, trying to monopolize a sexual partner was definitely a sin. Which was enough of a problem all by itself, seeing as she had no experience in sharing.

She slowly disentangled herself from Kislan's embrace. "I didn't seek you out for this. I wanted to ask you about something I don't understand, something that might help me understand more."

"Yes?"

"In your creation myth, all the men are killed in the war between the Kishudiu and the Tusalis. But how could the women have started a new society without men? Is there any explanation in the myth for that?"

Kislan shrugged. "What explanation is needed? Yes, all of the men died; the warriors, *zhamhain-yanar,* but that is not everyone."

"'Hainyan'? I don't know that word yet. What

does it mean?"

"'Hainyan' is the word for the man when a man and a woman are together as a family."

"But I thought that was 'maishal'?"

"No, no. 'Hainyan' is an old word. For the way it used to be. Much as you told us about the ways in the land you come from." He seemed to be both repelled and fascinated by the thought, and Toni remembered how he and Anash and Thuyene could only understand the marriages of Terran and Martian culture in terms of possession.

If Toni was right, and "yanaru" was the word for woman in Alnar ag Eshmaled, then the root of "hainyan" could be "over-woman."

A husband — like on the world she came from.

"But that still doesn't explain how the Mejan came to be," she said.

"They made their slaves their husbands." This time he used the word "maishal."

Toni stared at him. The women had owned the men when they first came here. *Their* language had possessive cases, the men's language — the language which had evolved from the dialect of the slaves? — did not. And the pirates to the east, the men who kept slaves — was the word for pirate perhaps the original word for men in the women's language?

That would explain why Toni had thought they'd been discussing "pirates" when she asked if she could learn their language.

Suddenly things started coming together for her like a landslide. And she was almost certain Repnik had figured it out — which was why he was doing his best to hinder their research.

Because he couldn't be chief linguist on a planet where the chief language was a women's language.

Then the thought occurred to her: what had really happened to Landra Saleh?

She pushed away from Kislan. "I must speak with Repnik."

"Why?"

"I think I know now why he was trying to forbid me from talking to the women."

"He did that?"

"Yes."

"But how can he have the authority? Authority belongs to the mother." *Tandarish derdesh kanezha tajanar.* He used the attitude particle "der-" for "a fact that cannot be denied."

Toni stared at him, her mind racing. *Authority belongs to the mother.* Tandarish - tajanar. "Tan" and "tajan" could well have the same root, which would mean the authority of the mother was even embedded in the word itself.

She pulled a notebook and pen out of her shoulder bag, sat down on one of the chairs, and began jotting down the possible cognates with the women's language, along with the old word for husband. And slave. She was trying to come up with a cognate for the first half of the word "godent" when Kislan interrupted her.

"What are you doing?" he asked, sitting down in the chair next to her and peering over her shoulder.

She didn't have any words for writing in his language, so she tried to describe it. "I have an idea about the Language of the People, and I wanted to make the symbols for the words in my language before I forget."

"I have seen the men of the contact team do this before, but I thought it was something like painting." He laughed out loud. "I did not understand, none of us did. Among us, the men are not responsible for making *dalonesh*."

Toni wasn't familiar with the last word. "What does 'dalonesh' mean?"

Kislan shrugged. "Events, history, business —

anything that should be passed on."

Records. He was speaking of records.

But in order to have records, you had to have a written language.

"Rodela," Toni murmured to herself. They had been even more dense than she'd suspected. The crocheting the women did during the meetings she'd attended was *writing*, making the records of important assembleys, and who knew what else.

"Yes," Kislan said, his voice thoughtful. "You mean, among the people from the sky both men and women learn *rodela?*"

Both men and women learn crocheting, Toni's brain translated for her stubbornly, and she had to laugh.

Kislan started away, and she laid a hand on his forearm. "I am sorry, I meant no offense. Repnik had translated 'rodela' with a word for a hobby practiced mostly by women on the world where he comes from. The answer to your question is: yes, on the worlds I know, Earth, Mars, Jyuruk and Admetos, we all learn writing, men and women both."

"I have often thought it would be good to know, but men are not regarded as masculine if they learn *rodela*. It is not taught to us."

Men are not regarded as masculine if they learn cro-

cheting. Certainly not. That fit very well into the mind set the first contact team had brought with them to Christmas. But they were not talking about crocheting, they were talking about the power of passing on knowledge through the written word. In order for people of her cultural background to understand Kislan's statement, more than "rodela" would have to be changed. To get at the underlying attitude, the gender of the words would have to be changed as well: *Women are not regarded as feminine if they learn writing.*

That was the attitude that was behind what Kislan had said. He had not mentioned "rodela" like something he could easily do without, he had mentioned it with regret, like something denied to him. Even if the words were translated with their correct meanings, the sentence made no sense, at least not on any world in the Allied Interstellar Community. *Men are not regarded as masculine if they learn writing.*

"Is it forbidden?" Toni asked.

Kislan frowned, nodding. "It is not done. I know no man capable of *rodela.*"

Toni took a deep breath. Suddenly everything about the Mejan looked completely different. The world had tilted and turned upside-down, and now the Christmas tree was right-side up. She couldn't believe how blind they had been, how blind *she* had been.

Except, perhaps, Repnik.

Of course, the first contact team had been plagued by bad luck from the start — or was it? — with no sociologist, no one to talk to the women, and a xenolinguist who was deliberately deceiving everyone. But that did not excuse the extent of the misunderstanding, and it certainly did not excuse her own mistakes. She'd felt that something was off, but she had allowed her own inherited attitudes to keep her from figuring out what it was.

"And the wall hangings?" she asked, beginning to pace. "What are those?"

He shrugged. "Genealogies, histories, famous stories. *Fashar.*"

Documents, books perhaps. Another word which would have to be changed. Translated as "lace" in the present dictionary. The books, the writing, it had been there right in front of their faces all this time. This had implications for their whole analysis of the language.

She stopped and turned to face him. "I have to speak with Repnik."

"Dai eden mashal." Which meant the same as "good" but was expressed in verb form. And if she had said the same thing to another woman, it would have been "dai desh mashal."

But after this, she would probably never trust her knowledge of another language again.

[17]

The Story of the Young Poet
Recorded 30.09.157 by Landra Saleh, retranslated 06.12.157 (local AIC date) by Antonia Donato.

As long as she could remember, Zhaykair had only one dream - to become the greatest poet the Mejan had ever known. All young girls are taught the basics of writing, but Zhaykair would not stop at that. She begged the women of her village to teach her their way with words, the patterns they created, and she quickly found the most talented writer among them. Saymel did not belong to Zhaykair's house, but the families reached an agreement, and the little girl was allowed to learn from Saymel, although the job of Zhaykair's house was raising cattle.

But before she had seen nine summers, Zhaykair had learned all Saymel had to teach her. She begged her clan to allow her to go to the city of Edaru, where the greatest poets of the Mejan lived. Her mothers and fathers did not want to send her away, but Saymel, who could best judge the talent of the young girl, persuaded them to inquire if the house of Mihkal would be willing to take her on.

The elders sent a messenger to the Mihkal with some of Zhaykair's poems. They had feared being ridiculed for their presumption, but the messenger returned with an elder of the house of Mihkal to personally escort Zhaykair to the great city of Edaru.

Zhaykair soon learned all the Mihkal clan could teach her. Her poetry was in such great demand, and there were so many who wanted to learn from her, that she could soon found her own house. Her works now grace the walls of all the greatest families of the Mejan.

[18]

Toni found Repnik in the main square of Edaru, leaving the school of the house of Railiu, where boys memorized a wealth of Mejan legends and songs and were taught basic mathematics and biology and navigational skills.

But no crocheting.

"Sir!" Toni called out, rushing over to him. "I need to speak with you. Can we perhaps return to the contact house?"

"*You* can return to the contact house, Donato. I am going out to lunch with Sebair, the rector of the Railiu school."

Sebair strolled next to Repnik with his hand to his forehead, and Toni returned the gesture, greeting him less graciously than she should have.

"Sha bo sham, tajan," Sebair said in response, smiling despite her lack of manners.

"Mr. Repnik," Toni persisted. "I really need to speak with you. It's very important."

"I am sure you think it is. But you have a job to do, and what you have to tell me can wait until I get back to the lab."

Toni took a deep breath. "I know. What you've been trying to hide."

Repnik's stride faltered, but his confidence did-n't, at least not as far she could tell. "I have no idea what you're talking about."

"I know that as far as the Mejan are concerned, I am the head of this contact team. And I know that they *do* have a system of writing."

Repnik stopped in his tracks. "You know *what?*"

So it seemed he hadn't gotten that far. He wasn't a good enough actor to fake that stare of surprise. He knew the women were the ones with the final say around here, but not what the crocheting really was. Toni felt a surge of satisfaction.

"And I also know that you've been trying to hinder the research of the first contact team."

An angry flush covered the chief linguist's face.

"Ms. Donato, you are hallucinating."

"I don't think so. So don't you want to know what the system of writing is?"

Repnik snorted. "There is none. I knew before you came to Christmas that a woman dealing with a woman's language would lead to problems."

Finally, Toni could no longer control her temper. "Obviously not as many problems as a man dealing with a men's language," she spat out.

She saw his hand come up as if the moment were being replayed in slow motion. She knew it meant he was about to slap her, but she was too surprised to react. From that observing place in her mind, she saw Sebair start forward and try to stop Repnik, but then the flat of his palm met her cheek, the sting of pain sending tears to her eyes.

She lifted her own palm to cover the spot. Suddenly, utter silence reigned in the main square, everyone gaping at her and her boss. Then, just as suddenly, chaos broke out. The men who had been going about their business only minutes before converged upon Repnik and wrestled him to the ground.

Toni stood frozen, staring at the scene in front of her. Repnik had struck a mother.

The old man struggled beneath the three young

men who held him down. "What is the meaning of this?" he yelled in Alnar ag Ledar.

Suddenly Lanrhel was there next to them. Toni wondered when he had joined the fray.

"Let him rise," the Councilor said.

The voluntary guards pulled Repnik to his feet, and Lanrhel faced him. "You know enough of our laws to know that to strike a mother means you must be returned to the sea."

Repnik wrenched one arm free and pointed at Toni. "*She* is no mother."

Lanrhel didn't even bother to answer, turning instead to Toni. "Tajan, do you need assistance?"

She was too confused to come up with the right gesture and shook her head. "No, it's nothing. Let him go, please."

A firm hand took her elbow. "Come." *Anash.*

"But Repnik ..."

"Come. He must go with Lanrhel now."

Toni allowed herself to be led away to the common house and a small, private room. A basin of water was brought, and Anash pushed her into a chair and bathed her stinging cheek gently.

"You won't really throw him out to sea, will you?" Toni finally asked.

"I do not know yet what we will do. We have a dilemma."

They certainly did. Toni didn't even know if Repnik could swim. And if he could, he wouldn't be allowed to swim to shore. She didn't like him, but — a death sentence for a slap? "You can't give him back to the sea. He is not from this world. Where he's from, it's not a crime to slap a woman."

"Then it should be," Anash said grimly.

Anash was defending her, but it didn't feel like it. "Don't do this to him, please."

"How can you defend him after all the disrespect he has shown you?"

If Toni hadn't felt so horrible, she almost would have been tempted to laugh. That was the kind of reasoning shown by aristocracies and intolerant ruling powers throughout the histories of all the worlds she had ever visited. Disrespect as a capital crime.

Repnik hadn't been right to try to keep the truth from the first contact team, but he hardly deserved to walk the plank. Until this morning, she'd thought these women needed to be defended from the likes of Repnik. Now everything was on its head, everything.

As if to prove her point, Kislan entered the room, shutting the door gently behind him. He stared at her expectantly, and she finally remembered to greet him.

"Sha bo sham, Kislan."

"Sha bo sham, Toni." He approached and gave her a kiss, right in front of Anash.

His clan knew. They must have given him to her. *Like a present.* She was the visiting dignitary, and he was her whore. Had he thrown himself in her way willingly, or had he been forced to seek her out?

Toni pushed herself out of the chair, away from Kislan, and wandered over to the window. The central square of Edaru was unusually quiet for this time of day, just before the midday meal. People stood in small groups of two or three, speaking with earnest faces, spreading the news. By evening, the whole city would know that a man of the people from the sky had committed a grave crime against the sole woman of the contact team. If nothing was done, not only would Anash's authority be undermined, the first contact team would be seen as lawless and immoral.

She glanced up, above the rooftops of the buildings on the other side of the square, to the faint daytime hint of the lacy patterns in the sky, formed by the rings of Christmas.

The sky.

The old man wouldn't thank her, but she might have a way to save Repnik, keep him from being thrown into the ocean, and send him home safely.

"I have an idea," she breathed. "Criminals are returned to the sea, because that is where they are from, yes?"

Anash shook her head, watching Toni carefully.

"But the people of the first contact team do not come from the sea, they come from the sky."

"You are right," the older woman said. "This might be a solution."

Toni was the visiting dignitary, she had to remember that. "It is the only solution we can consider," she said in what she hoped was a voice of command.

Anash gazed at her as an equal. "Then we will give him back to the sky."

The ceremony took place on a sunny but cool afternoon three days later. Before arrangements could be made with the *Penthesilea*, they had to wait until the ship made contact itself. The taciturn Moshofski handled that end once Ainsworth overrode Repnik's commands, while Toni spent her time at the house of Ishel and in consultations with Lanrhel — aside from the one-sided shouting matches with Repnik, who was being kept under guard in the common house. Repnik had made it very clear that he intended to take Toni to interstellar court on charges of mutiny and conspiracy.

And if AIRA believed him, she was saving him to dig her own grave.

A construction resembling a pier was hastily built on a plain outside of town, between Edaru and the landing base. Although it was something of a trek for the town residents, several thousand people had made the trip to see Repnik returned to the sky.

With his head shaved, the old xenolinguist looked even older, gaunt and bare and bitter. Toni wished she didn't have to watch, let alone participate. The rest of the first contact team had elected to stay at home.

With a guard on either side, Repnik was accompanied down the waterless pier, Anash, Toni, and Thuyene a few paces behind. A shuttle from the *Penthesilea* waited at the end, Lanrhel and Ainsworth beside the door. Finally Repnik and his guards reached the councilor, and Lanrhel announced in his booming voice, "Mukhaired ag Repnik bonaashali der-ladesh." *Repnik's shame will now certainly be purged.* He then ordered the older man to strip. When Repnik refused, his guards stripped him forcibly.

Toni looked away. His humiliation was painful to see, his skinny, white flesh hanging loosely on his bones. He would hate her for the rest of his life, and she could hardly blame him.

Then Anash's hand on her elbow was urging her forward, pressing a bit of lace into her hand. A written record of Repnik's time on Christmas. Toni took a deep breath, looked up, and flung the *fashar* through the open doors of the shuttle.

Ainsworth nodded a curt goodbye, turned, and followed Repnik. The doors whisked shut, and the shuttle lifted off the ground.

After the ceremony, Anash led her to a small carriage to take her back to town. She was no longer surprised that the driver was Kislan again, and only a little surprised that Anash didn't join them.

Kislan was her present, after all.

If only Toni knew what to say, what to feel. He was still just as handsome, but she wasn't drawn to him in the same way as she had been only days before. She did not like what it said about herself, that she suddenly saw him so differently. Now he was a supplicant, whereas before he had been exotic and distant, a man of good standing in a powerful clan, nearly unattainable.

And she found that she didn't have the same feelings for someone who had been given to her as a welcoming gift.

"What is wrong, Toni?" Kislan asked gently after she hadn't spoken for minutes. His pronunciation of her name was a little like that of her Italian grandmother, and she had an odd impulse to cry.

"I don't know. I can't figure anything out."

"I thought you did not like Repnik?"

"No."

"Then why are you upset?"

"Things are so much stranger here than I thought. I'm confused. I need to think things out."

"And thinking things out includes me, yes?"

For a moment, Toni couldn't answer. "Yes."

Kislan looked away from her, concentrating on the road, and didn't speak again.

She arrived at Contact House One just as the lacy show of evening was beginning, her heart and mind a mess. The world was on its head and there were holes in the sky.

At the sound of hooves and wheels on the cobblestones, Sam, Jackson and Moshofski came out of the door to the courtyard, their expressions solemn.

Sam helped her down. "Ainsworth contacted us from the shuttle. They had to sedate Repnik."

Toni closed her eyes briefly. "I'm so sorry."

"No need, Donato," Jackson said. "Repnik was deliberately hindering AIRA work. And your plan kept him from being thrown into the sea."

"We've started to question what really happened to Landra," Moshofski added.

"I've been wondering about that too."

"We mentioned our suspicions to Ainsworth, and there will be an investigation," Jackson said.

She could only hope their suspicions were unfounded.

But Jackson wasn't done. "Given our new insights into the social structures on Christmas, you're to head the first contact team in future when dealing with the Mejan."

A smile touched Moshofski's serious features. "But in the lab, I'm to be the boss. Seniority, you know."

She could hardly believe it. "Certainly."

"Sam baked a cake to celebrate the two promotions," Jackson said. "Shall we test his talents?"

"I'll follow you in a minute."

The three men filed back into the contact house, and she came around the carriage to Kislan's side. "I never wanted to hurt you."

He gazed at her, not answering.

Toni looked away, at the sky above, the fabulous sunset over Edaru. "I'm sorry. I do not know what to think now. I will come see you again soon, and we can talk. Perhaps I can teach you our way of writing."

His eyes lit up. "Yes." He placed his free hand on her shoulder and nodded at the sky. "It's beautiful, isn't it?" *It is-in-a-state-of-beauty, yes?*

Toni shook her head. "Yes."

END

Author's Note

The inspiration for *Looking Through Lace* might come as something of a surprise: it was the mangling and misuse of German in a story I read in a speculative fiction magazine. I didn't learn German until I was in high school, and I have no deep-seated loyalty to the language or anything like that. What irritated me was the assumption on the part of the author that the only thing necessary to create some German sentences for local color was a dictionary.

I knew then that I had to write a story in which the sheer complexity of language was a central element.

Creating the languages of Kailazh was more work than the actual writing of the story itself. I started reading up on conlangs (constructed languages), subscribed to mailing lists, brushed up on historical linguistics, and learned a lot about how languages develop over time. Many a boring conference was spent working on the grammar and vocabulary of *Alnar ag Eshmaled*.

I want to thank the people who read and critiqued *Looking Through Lace* before its initial publication in 2003. Among the fellow writers who helped me get the story into shape are Tamela Viglione, S. K. S. Perry, Larry West, Steve Ramey, Laura Fischer, Marsha Sisolak, Celia Marsh, Steve Nagy, Karen Over, Jon Paradise, and A. L. Hicks.

I was thrilled when Gardner Dozois bought it for *Asimov's* its first time out. I was afraid it was such an ungainly length, and me so new to the SF scene, that I would have a terrible time finding a home for it.

A word of thanks also to my Italian editor Silvio Sosio of Delos Books for choosing the story for translation, which in turn led to the Premio Italia award for *Looking Through Lace*, and an excellent time as Guest of Honor in Fiuggi the following year.

Finally, thanks go to Lou Harper for the stunning new cover.

Thank you all very much!

Ruth Nestvold

Excerpt from

Beyond the Waters of the Word

Looking Through Lace 2

The docks of Edaru rarely slept. While it would not be a ship captain's choice to make port at night, tides and winds had moods of their own, not to be controlled by the captain of a sailing vessel.

This particular ship had come to port at night. Even though the hour was late, it was best to count and secure the cargo immediately. Kislan was inspecting the shipment of bowls of carved and polished eyliu shells from Melpaan and sturdy coils of rope from Sithray by the light of torches held high by his assistants, three young men of his house.

He had begun to use the drawing-writing for keeping records. He held a thin block of wood with a piece of parchment (such as was usually used for drawing maps) affixed to it in one hand, and an implement Toni called a "pensil" in the other — very different than the needle and fine yarn the Mejan women used for writing. With this type of writing, he could record many more details than were possible with the simple knots the men of the Thirteen Cities used. While he wrote down wares and amounts and qualities, another assistant made knots for the cargo in the traditional way.

The wind from the sea picked up and Kislan had to hold down the edge of the parchment with one hand. Hair laced with braids of multicolored threads whipped around his face. He tucked the *pensil* into a cord on the writing block and pulled his hair back from his forehead, holding it in place as he looked up.

Toni was hurrying along the docks toward him.

His reaction was immediate, and it didn't help that he cursed himself for it. To show desire for a woman who had given no indication that she wanted a man's attentions was an act of shame, doubly so if the woman was not of a man's house.

The second didn't apply to the ambassador, however, since his house had designated him as her gift — which she had rejected.

When the men around him noticed the direction of his gaze, they too turned. At the sight of the woman from the stars, they flowed away like a wave leaving shore.

Toni didn't seem aware of the interpersonal dynamics of the men on the docks, heading for him unerringly in that determined, single-minded way she had. The thought made him smile. And the closer she came, the wider his smile grew.

When she reached him, she took his arm, making the young men behind him gasp. It was an exceedingly impolite gesture between adults, but Kislan could see her expression now —urgent, fearful even.

"Sha bo sham, Kislan."

"Sha bo sham, Toni."

"Can we talk in your office?"

"If you could wait a moment, tajan? I must finish here first." She seemed impatient at the delay, but there wasn't anything he could do about it.

He completed his inspection of the cargo, aware of the woman from the stars the whole time. Finally, his job done, he turned to her. "I am at your service now."

She nodded curtly, and he paused for a moment until he remembered that in her culture, the gesture meant the opposite from his — nodding was for agreement. The ambassador must be very distracted if she forgot to shake her head; as if she had forgotten she was among the Mejan.

"What is it, Toni?" he asked as they hurried along the dark street to the low building holding the offices of the factors. Stars flickered between the black streaks of the planet's rings in the sky above them. That the lace in the sky was caused by rings around his planet was another thing Kislan had not known until Toni showed him pictures from far beyond his world.

"Not here," she said.

Kislan was starting to get worried. The streets were empty, there was no one near, and still she did not want to tell him why she'd sought him out.

When they entered the office, his house brother Zhoran was still there, working by the light of a lamp at his elbow, practicing the drawing-writing Kislan had been teaching him. Zhoran was captain of an Ishel merchant ship and wore the same colors as Kislan in his braids, those of the houses of Ishel and Kirtanar. But more than that, Zhoran was a friend such as few men had.

Zhoran rose at Toni's entrance and lifted the back of his hand to his forehead in a sign of respect, waiting for her to speak first, as was proper.

Toni returned the gesture. "Sha bo sham, Zhoran."

"Sha bo sham, tajan."

"Would you leave me alone with Kislan for a moment, please?"

"As you will."

Zhoran gathered up the parchment and brushes he had been using. "I will come to you again tomorrow evening for more instruction?" he said to Kislan.

Toni left him no time to answer. "I wouldn't recommend it," she said. She indicated the parchment Zhoran held. "This is what I came to speak with Kislan about."

"Then perhaps Zhoran should remain?" Kislan suggested.

Again Toni nodded, forgetting for the second time in the space of a short walk where among the stars she found herself. She began to pace the small office with long, determined strides, those strides that were among the many things Kislan recalled whenever she ghosted through his waking dreams.

"I overheard a conversation tonight, at a gathering of representatives from the Thirteen Cities." Her voice was like a calm sea far from shore, with barely a wave to disrupt it — but with danger lurking in its depths. "If I understood right, several of the women were discussing the *problem* that increasing numbers of men in Edaru are learning to use drawing-writing — and what to do about it."

For a while, the only sound in the room was that of Toni's footfalls on the stone floor.

"Do about it?" Kislan finally repeated.

"Yes." The woman from the stars stopped pacing and faced him. "I fear for you."

"Why?"

"While this culture has no taboos against men using drawing-writing —"

Zhoran snorted, and for the first time since she had sought Kislan out this night, Toni smiled. "I know, I know. How could there be a taboo regarding something that doesn't exist in Kailazh culture?" Her expression grew serious again. "But the women I overheard were talking about the disruption of social structures if men developed a system of writing of their own. Someone even suggested it might be a misdeed similar to that of a man trying to learn the Language of the House."

Kislan stared at her, not knowing what to say. *Alnar ag Eshmaled*, the Language of the House, was spoken only by women, and it was forbidden for men to learn it. Those who repeatedly tried after being warned were returned to the sea — just as were men who struck a woman or stole from another house or murdered a brother.

"What are you saying?" Zhoran said.

"I'm saying that they may be changing the laws to make drawing-writing a crime." She took Kislan's hands. "And making you a criminal. I'm sorry, I'm so sorry."

End excerpt

ABOUT THE AUTHOR

Ruth Nestvold's fiction has appeared in numerous markets, including *Asimov's, F&SF, Strange Horizons, Realms of Fantasy,* and Gardner Dozois's *Year's Best Science Fiction.* Her stories have been nominated for the Nebula, Tiptree, and Sturgeon Awards. In 2007, the Italian translation of *Looking Through Lace* won the "Premio Italia" award for best international work. Her novel *Yseult* appeared in German translation as *Flamme und Harfe* with Random House Germany and has since been translated into Dutch and Italian.

http://www.ruthnestvold.com

CPSIA information can be obtained
at www.ICGtesting.com
Printed in the USA
LVHW042146111020
668544LV00001B/259